THIS WALKER BOOK BELONGS TO:

_____

_____

_____

_____

For the boys of
St Mary's Primary School,
Newcastle, Co. Down

M.W.

For Mrs Window

D.M.

First published 1988 by
Walker Books Ltd
87 Vauxhall Walk
London SE11 5HJ

Text © 1988 Martin Waddell
Illustrations © 1988 Dom Mansell

First printed 1988
Printed in Hong Kong by Sheck Wah Tong Printing Press Ltd

British Library Cataloguing in Publication Data
Waddell, Martin
Great Gran Gorilla to the rescue.
I. Title   II. Mansell, Dom
823'. 914 [J] PZ7

ISBN 0-7445-0752-9
ISBN 0-7445-0754-5 pbk

GREAT GRAN GORILLA
GORILLA
to the Rescue

Written by

MARTIN WADDELL

Illustrated by

DOM MANSELL

WALKER BOOKS

LONDON

The Gran Gang are in the snow.

Gran Brown is feeding the robin on her head. Gran Smith is being gorgeous and Gran Jones has the ammunition. Great Gran Gorilla is the deadly snowballer. The Gran Gang's spies are going OOOOH! EHH! UFFF! AAAAA! and OOOOO!

Then, somewhere else...

"Help!" cried the little girl.

The Gran Gang's spy has spotted her!

Can you spot the spy?

"Little girl in frozen river! Come quick!"

Gran Brown got the message
on her hearing aid,
and the Gran Gang
got going.

Here is the Gran Gang getting going.

VAROOOOOOOOOOOOOOMMM!

The motor bike is in the snow-drift, and the Grans are in the snow.

The bright yellow legs belong to Gran Smith. The smart blue wellies belong to Gran Brown. The other four legs are attached to Great Gran Gorilla and Gran Jones. The great big boots are on Great Gran Gorilla's great big feet.

"The Grans are beaten this time!" cried all the people. BUT...

"Trolley boggan, girls!" cried Great Gran Gorilla.

This is the Grans making a trolley-boggan jump. But...

SPLOSH!

The trolley boggan has bust apart. The Grans are tumbling over in the snow.

"Get it together, girls!" cried Great Gran Gorilla.

The Grans have grabbed each other. They are a GRAN BALL now.

"Roll it, girls!" cried Great Gran Gorilla.

The Grans are rolling, and the Gran Ball
is getting bigger...
and B I G G E R...
and B I G G E R.
So big that you can't see Gran Smith and
Gran Brown and Gran Jones at all.

The umbrellascope belongs to Great
Gran Gorilla. She is in the middle of the
Gran Ball, heading for the river.

CRUNCH-CRACK-SPLOSH!

The Gran Ball has splonked into the frozen river. The little girl has splonked out.

The Grans are under the four hats.
All the people are cheering the Grans.

The big lollies are the Grans.
The Gran Gang's spies are wheeling
them home.

The Grans have melted.

The people in the flat downstairs don't know why there is water coming through their ceiling.

They are sailing on their sofa.

The canary is seasick.

But it is all right. Great Gran Gorilla
has rescued them.

The three Grans have blue noses
and cold toes and bad coughs. They will

get better soon because Great Gran Gorilla
is looking after them. She always does.

MORE WALKER PAPERBACKS

PICTURE BOOKS
For 4 to 6-Year-Olds

Sarah Hayes
The Walker Fairy Tale Library
BOOKS ONE TO SIX
Six collections of favourite stories

Helen Craig
Susie and Alfred
THE NIGHT OF THE PAPER BAG MONSTERS
A WELCOME FOR ANNIE

Jane Asher & Gerald Scarfe
The Moppy Stories
MOPPY IS HAPPY   MOPPY IS ANGRY

PICTURE BOOKS
For 6 to 10-Year-Olds

Martin Waddell
& Joseph Wright
Little Dracula
LITTLE DRACULA'S FIRST BITE
LITTLE DRACULA'S CHRISTMAS
LITTLE DRACULA AT THE SEASIDE
LITTLE DRACULA GOES TO SCHOOL

Patrick Burston
& Alastair Graham
Which Way?
THE PLANET OF TERROR
THE JUNGLE OF PERIL

E.J. Taylor
Biscuit, Buttons and Pickles
IVY COTTAGE   GOOSE EGGS

Quentin Blake
& Michael Rosen
Scrapbooks
UNDER THE BED
HARD-BOILED LEGS
SMELLY JELLY SMELLY FISH
SPOLLYOLLYDIDDLYTIDDLYITIS

Peter Dallas-Smith
& Peter Cross
TROUBLE FOR TRUMPETS

Adrian Mitchell
& Patrick Benson
THE BARON RIDES OUT

David Lloyd
& Charlotte Voake
THE RIDICULOUS STORY OF
GAMMER GURTON'S NEEDLE

Selina Hastings
& Juan Wijngaard
SIR GAWAIN AND THE LOATHLY LADY